Good things happen
from a little remembering.

Hanukkah, Shmanukkah!

BY

ESMÉ RAJI CODELL

ILLUSTRATED BY

LEUYEN PHAM

Hyperion Books for Children/New York

What a *punim*! Thanks to Johnno Freeman.
—*E. R. C.*

Much thanks goes to Gratia Meyer for her insights, and to
Ruben Hickman for the loan of his precious image.
—*L. P.*

Text copyright © 2005 by Esmé Raji Codell
Illustrations copyright © 2005 by LeUyen Pham

The rabbi's quote on p. 24, "Give me your tired, your poor, your huddled masses yearning to
breathe free," is from "The New Colossus" by Emma Lazarus, written in 1883 and carved into
the pedestal of the Statue of Liberty.

The passages in the author's note on pp. 48–49 are reprinted from pp. 59, 61, and 84 of *A Bintel Brief:
Sixty Years of Letters from the Lower East Side to the Jewish Daily Forward*, edited and translated by
Isaac Metzker, published by Schocken Books, New York.

Printed in Singapore

First Edition
1 3 5 7 9 10 8 6 4 2

This book is set in Parkinson Roman.
Reinforced binding

ISBN 0-7868-5179-1
Library of Congress Cataloging-in-Publication Data on file.

Visit www.hyperionbooksforchildren.com

To my mother and father
—*E. R. C.*

This book is dedicated to the fair Sabrina,
the new Rose in our family
—*L. P.*

"Shmendrick, *pick up the pace or I'll give you such a zetz!*"

Old man Scroogemacher was as sour as a pickle and had a tongue like horseradish. He would lash out at all the workers in his waistcoat factory.

"*Shvieg!* No talking during work hours!"

"*Shmendrick,* pick up the pace or I'll give you such a *zetz*!"

"What's the matter with you, you greenhorn klutz! If you ruin the work, you'll pay for it!"

Poor Gerstein turned as white as a ghost. Pay for it? With five mouths at home to feed, like baby birds?

But this is how Scroogemacher talked, *geshray*ing from sunrise to sunset. *Gevalt!* There are only so many hours in the day, but Scroogemacher even knew how to fix that.

"Adjust the clock," he ordered his foreman, who went behind the wall and turned a small dial. Slowly the minute hand went backward. Five minutes... Ten minutes...

"Oh, Uncle," said Moshe. "Not tonight. Please, it's the last night of Hanukkah. Let them go home at a decent hour."

"What? Are they going to be late for a game of dreidel? And what do they have to gamble, the *shmattes* on their backs? Hanukkah, shmanukkah," Scroogemacher said. "It's just another night to me."

"Maybe it's more to them," Moshe pointed out.

"Them, shmem." Old Scroogemacher waved his hand. "Always with the *them*. What do you care about *them*, you free-thinking young fool?"

"Some of them have children," said Moshe.

"Children, shmildren," grunted Scroogemacher. "So let them work to feed them."

"But some of them *are* children." Moshe followed Scroogemacher, who turned around and narrowed his eyes.

"Nephew," he said in a low, weary voice tinged with vinegar.

"Hanukkah, shmanukkah," Scroogemacher said. "It's just another night to me."

"You've got a lot of *chutzpah*. I bought your ticket here to the *Goldeneh Medineh* not so you could follow me around the floor *hok*ing my *chainik*, but to learn the trade and maybe someday take over for me, like a son. Life here is hard work and they know it, so why do you cry for them instead of enjoying your own privileges? If you weren't my nephew . . ."

"I'd be one of them," Moshe finished. "I'd be working late on this night of miracles."

Scroogemacher looked out over his workers, their bony shoulders hunched, their heads bent, faces pale, their eyes fluttering over muddy, sleepless half-circles. And guess what Scroogemacher said?

That's right. "Miracles, shmiracles."

"I think it would be a miracle if you would act like a *mensch*," grumbled Moshe, but luckily Scroogemacher didn't hear him. The hum of the sewing machines was too loud.

Past the tenements old Scroogemacher's carriage rolled, leaving long trails in the slush. His nose wrinkled at the smell of laundry water, boiled cabbage, and horses. The moon hung thin and emaciated, yellow like a fingernail cutting, overseeing the ghostly lines of laundry. It is a chilly night, Scroogemacher thought, shivering beneath his coat. Did Moshe say he would be home late? I think tonight I will go straight to bed.

Past the tenements old Scroogemacher's carriage rolled, leaving long trails in the slush.

But when he crawled into his bed, Scroogemacher had a funny feeling in his *kishkes*. It didn't go away, even with seltzer. That *farshtunkener* butcher sold me bad meat, thought Scroogemacher.

"It's not the meat," came a voice.

"A *gonif*!" cried Scroogemacher.

But when he sat up, he saw a rabbi, hardly tall enough to see over the foot of his bed, but handsomely dressed in black with a silver tallis, and cheeks as round and red as apples.

"Don't ask me for alms. I put in the *tzedakah* box already," Scroogemacher lied.

But the little rabbi only shook his head and chuckled.

"*Oy*, Scroogemacher," said the rabbi. "You are such a *shtunk*."

"How do you know my name? Who let you in?" demanded Scroogemacher.

A rabbi... dressed in black with a silver tallis, and cheeks as round and red as apples.

"I heard you like to *patshke* with clocks," said the little man. "It so happens that I do, too. I am the Rabbi of Hanukkah Past, and I have arrived to *shlep* you to *hotzeplotz* and back so you will see that Hanukkah is nothing to sneeze at."

"Hanukkah, shmanukkah," replied Scroogemacher. "Probably I ate too much garlic and onions. I'm seeing a little *dybbuk* at the foot of my bed. You let yourself in, so see yourself out." He pulled the covers over his head. But even when he closed his eyes, the rabbi appeared, as if in a dream. When Scroogemacher tried to awaken, it seemed as though he couldn't.

What spell is this? he wondered.

"So, Scroogemacher, do you not know from lighting a menorah? One candle

for each of the eight nights of Hanukkah, and of course the ninth candle, the *shammes*."

"Of course I know the story of Hanukkah. What do you take me for, a nincompoop?"

"So, give me a history lesson."

Scroogemacher sighed. Faster is better, he thought, and talk is cheap. So he began.

"Two thousand years ago, give or take a few, *meshuggehs* captured the holy temple, made such a mess."

"Like this?" the rabbi asked. Suddenly, all around the two men, soldiers of old appeared, smashing furniture with great steely blows from their swords. Flames crawled up the walls, and black smoke billowed. Through the darkness, Scroogemacher could see the soldiers pillage the great temple, gathering the gold.

Rocks and arrows rained down through the air.

"*Vey iz mir,* what place is this?" Scroogemacher said, cowering behind an overturned table.

"The desecrated temple," said the rabbi. "Mid-desecration. Front row, center."

"*Gevalt!* What a *tuml!* How can this be? Rabbi, we must flee King Antiochus's soldiers!"

"Nothing doing. They can't see us, my friend. So go on with your story. You were saying?"

"The Jews fought back." Scroogemacher trembled.

"*Nu?* Like this?" At once, men in tunics poured in, howling and wielding swords and sticks. Rocks and arrows rained down through the air, with the groans of men taking their last breath and dropping like lead against the stone floor. Scroogemacher found himself screaming, but stopped, awestruck, when there entered a man who moved calmly through the terror and laid low his enemy left and right.

"Judah Maccabee." The Rabbi of Hanukkah Past smiled. "*Maccabee* means 'hammer,' as you know, being such a smarty-pants. He was the mighty

"Judah Macabee." The Rabbi of Hanukkah Past smiled.

son of Mattathais. When the soldiers came to Modin, they built an altar. Mattathais was ordered to bow down before a statue of a Greek idol and sacrifice a pig to it. Not too kosher. So, do you remember what happened next?"

"Mattathais opened a mouth," said Scroogemacher. "He said he would never worship idols, and his five sons attacked the soldiers. The villagers joined the *mishegas*, and the soldiers retreated. But they would return, and the Maccabees fled to caves in the mountains, where they formed an army and learned to fight."

"All from someone standing up to a *makher*!" The rabbi's eyes grew wide, and the vision of the temple dimmed and faded. "So, what would have happened if old Gerstein had stood up to you when you docked his pay, I wonder? Maybe you'd find a hundred hammers on your head?"

"One has nothing to do with the other!" shouted Scroogemacher.

"Who says one has to do with the other? A man can't wonder about hammers? So go on. You haven't told me the end of your story."

"The Maccabees won the war and returned to the land of Judea. When they returned to the temple, it was all *farpatshket*, the soldiers had made such a mess. There was so much work to do, but there was only enough oil to last for one night. They say it is a miracle that the oil lasted for eight, and so there are eight candles in a menorah and one *shammes*, to remember the rededication of the temple won back by the Maccabees."

But the rabbi was hardly listening. He was looking at his watch. "He should be here by now."

"Who?"

"Ah, here he is. Scroogemacher, meet the Rabbi of Hanukkah Present. Rabbi, this is Mr. Scroogemacher. You will excuse me for running off, but you see, I'm late for latkes. My wife makes the best latkes. But she will understand why I am not on time. Everyone works late here in the New World, right, Scroogemacher?" He winked, and before Scroogemacher could answer, the little rabbi was gone.

"Your mouth is hanging open," remarked the new rabbi, tall and pointed as a sewing needle. "You must be hungry. Don't worry. I know where we can get a nosh."

"Your mouth is hanging open," remarked the new rabbi, tall and pointed as a sewing needle.

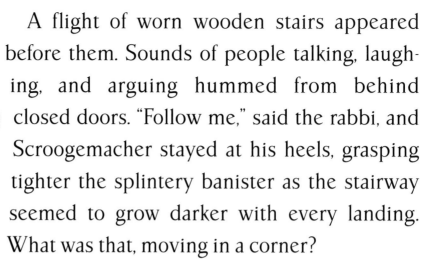

A flight of worn wooden stairs appeared before them. Sounds of people talking, laughing, and arguing hummed from behind closed doors. "Follow me," said the rabbi, and Scroogemacher stayed at his heels, grasping tighter the splintery banister as the stairway seemed to grow darker with every landing. What was that, moving in a corner?

"The cheaper flats are at the top," the rabbi explained. "Here we are."

"At last," huffed Scroogemacher. "So what devilish place is this, now?"

"Devilish! Why, Scroogemacher, it is the tenement of your own worker, Gerstein! Surely you remember him—you docked him two cents for a crooked hem only a few hours ago!"

"*Shvieg!*" ordered Scroogemacher. "Listen, someone is coming. Who knows what bad element frequents such a shoddy tenement at this time of night?"

"Oh, Scroogemacher," said the Rabbi of Hanukkah Present, laughing, "don't you recognize your own nephew?"

"What is that *mazik* doing here?" Scroogemacher jumped back into the shadows, but the rabbi reminded him that he was still invisible. Up the stairs came Moshe, bounding two at a time. In his arms were packages. He knocked on the door. Gerstein opened it and welcomed him with wide arms.

Up the stairs came Moshe, bounding two at a time. In his arms were packages.

He called out to announce Moshe, and what followed were warm shouts of greeting and the thunderous sound of *kinder* jumping up and down on the floorboards. Scroogemacher and the rabbi slipped inside before the door closed.

The apartment was barely two rooms with a single window looking out upon a wall of bricks. A draft lifted the ragged curtain strung across the pane. Beds were set abreast so that you couldn't even walk.

Though it was the middle of the night, everyone was awake: Mr. and Mrs. Gerstein with their older daughter and four small children, one still a baby on her mother's hip. Then there were the five boarders: a young man with his *bubbe*, and another man

wearing an undershirt, whose wife and small daughter clapped with glee at Moshe's arrival. At once the table was cleared of the hill of limp pants and waistcoats that had been brought home to work on, and the sewing machine and hot iron ushered off to a corner.

Moshe opened up his packages wrapped in newspaper from the butcher and baker and grocer with some ceremony. Each package met with noisy groans of delight. A loaf of bread! A roasted chicken! Smoked herring, fit for a czar! And pickles, yes, enough for each child to have their own! And could it be? A square of halvah, admired as if it were made of pure gold. Oh, what a happy Hanukkah! Mrs. Gerstein wept, and kissed Scroogemacher's nephew on both cheeks.

"Look at Gerstein's daughter," said the rabbi. "Lovely as a rose."

"What is this!" shrieked Scroogemacher. "I pay for his passage so he can gallivant with this crowd of riffraff!"

"Now, now," soothed the rabbi, his mouth full of herring. "Is that any way to talk about your nephew's future in-laws?"

"What!" exploded Scroogemacher.

"Look at Gerstein's daughter," said the rabbi. "Lovely as a rose."

"Rose, shmose." Scroogemacher snorted. "She's skinny as a weed, and with any luck, the wind will blow her away like one. I will fire her tomorrow, and Gerstein, too. Then we will see about getting my nephew a proper match!"

"Don't tell me you are against love, too," the rabbi said, tugging at his beard.

"Love is sweet, but with bread, it's better." Scroogemacher waved his hand.

"You would know, wouldn't you?" At once, the room went dark.

"Where did everybody go?" Scroogemacher whirled around. "Again with the dark?"

To Scroogemacher's amazement, the rabbi opened his waistcoat and pulled out a golden menorah. "Ahh," he groaned, "finally. It was giving me such a cramp, you wouldn't believe. Care to join me in the prayer?"

"It's an Old World tradition, and I left the old for the new," Scroogemacher said. "But do as you please. What's it to me?"

The rabbi nodded and, taking the *shammes*, he lit each candle and recited the ancient lines. The words and notes plucked at

"It is the new crop of your workers . . . crossing the Atlantic as we speak."

Scroogemacher's heart like the strains of a fiddle playing a familiar song, but he did not waver until the light cast by the candles revealed a ship's steerage.

Scroogemacher gasped. "Oh, Rabbi, don't make me relive this," he pleaded.

"You are not reliving anything," said the rabbi. "It is the new crop of your workers, Scroogemacher, crossing the Atlantic as we speak. It seems you will never run out of such poor wretches."

But Scroogemacher barely heard him, so carried off was he by his own memories. "Who could forget the passage? I was such a young man then, but I remember. Like dogs, crowded a thousand thick in a space that could barely hold a hundred. Three weeks of babies crying. No change of clothes, no place to do your private business, people sick all around. Onions would have smelled like perfume after breathing in the ethers of that Gehenna!"

"Like dogs, you say?" asked the rabbi. "And so you call your workers. Were they not so brave as yourself, to make such a treacherous journey?"

"To live in the *Goldeneh Medineh*, it is worth such peril." Scroogemacher straightened himself up. "These people coming have made the right decision, Rabbi. It is the land of opportunity and freedom. Is it not the world for Jews that Judah Macabee envisioned when he battled so bravely?"

"Perhaps it is for you." The rabbi shrugged. "But how about for your dogs, Mr. Scroogemacher? How about for your dogs?"

Scroogemacher's eyes surveyed the terrible scene. Beneath Scroogemacher's shoes, the boat swayed and lurched. Babies whined in an eerie rhythm that echoed through the hull. All around was a tangle, a human pile of scarves and suitcases and beating hearts.

"You look green, Scroogemacher." The rabbi touched his elbow. "Is the butcher's chicken bothering you again?"

Scroogemacher tripped unnoticed over the sprawl of sleeping cargo and climbed the stairs to the deck, just as crowded, but cut by the breeze of the night air. Air! He breathed it with great relief, and like the horde around him, he found himself with his head lifted toward the stars. The ship blew its great bass signal, and a cry rose from the crowd. Scroogemacher opened his eyes to see the torch of Lady Liberty, like a jewel in the distance.

"'Give me your tired, your poor, your huddled masses yearning to breathe free,'" recited the rabbi behind him.

Scroogemacher opened his eyes to see the torch of Lady Liberty, like a jewel in the distance.

"We were parted. I swore that I would send for her."

"I remember standing on this deck with my wife," Scroogemacher whispered. "She crossed the ocean twice, you know. Here, and then back again. When they checked her eyes, she had trachoma, the blinding disease, and got the chalk mark that meant she was forced to return. We were parted. I swore that I would send for her."

"So did you?"

"Why do you ask if you already know— to torture me, you *tsores monger*?" Scroogemacher bit his lip and wiped a tear from his eye before he could continue. "Man plans, and God laughs. Surely you know that, Rabbi! By the time I could save enough to send for her, it was too late. She had perished in the violence across the ocean. I gave the ticket to my sister's son—he was not even twelve then—so that the army shouldn't take him." He breathed a watery sigh. "And that's the way the cookie crumbled."

"It is good to hear your heart makes a noise besides the clunking of a sewing machine, Scroogemacher." The rabbi spoke gently. "He who has not tasted the bitter cannot know the sweet."

Scroogemacher could not help but smile at the rabbi. He looked at the rabbi's menorah until it seemed as if the glow of the statue's torch, growing ever nearer, was the light of the *shammes.*

The light seemed to grow brighter and brighter, and brighter still. Scroogemacher had to block the light with his hands to keep from being blinded. When at last he was able to see, he found himself sitting in a pile of snow.

"Hi," said a woman with curly hair and glasses, speaking from behind a scarf wrapped snugly around her neck. She held out her hand to him.

Scroogemacher allowed himself to be helped to his feet. He could not help but notice her gloves. "What fine leather," Scroogemacher said. The woman smiled and obligingly removed a glove for him to examine. "Look at this workman-ship! And your coat, is it wool? I'll give you twice whatever you paid," said Scroogemacher. The woman looked amused. "Three times, then!" he insisted.

"I am not a saleswoman, Mr. Scroogemacher. I am the Rabbi of Hanukkah Future."

Scroogemacher nearly fell back down into the snow laugh-ing. "I'm fainting!" he cried. "A woman rabbi! And I suppose women have the vote, too!"

"I am not a saleswoman, Mr. Scroogemacher. I am the Rabbi of Hanukkah Future."

"*Oy*, we had better start small." The rabbi rolled her eyes. "Did you have a nice trip?"

"I'm feeling a little *farblondzhet*, to tell you the truth," said Scroogemacher, sighing. "I'm beginning to wonder if I'll ever get home."

"You've been so patient, I promise, this is the last stop. I just thought there's something…or someone…you might want to see."

They walked into a school, invisible to all they encountered. Scroogemacher marveled at the brilliant glow of a flameless fire. "Electric lights," the rabbi explained. She led him to a room, and they floated through the door.

"So? A bunch of *vildekinder*. What do you want, a medal?

And just look at these no-goodnicks, at school in the middle of the day, while their parents toil! No wonder the girls have to wear pants! Even the teacher is wearing pants! Is this a school for farmers?"

The rabbi looked amused again.

"So now what's so funny?"

"In the future, children in America must go to school. Children are not allowed to work."

"School, shmool," scoffed Scroogemacher. "I know the law. The children must not be employed unless they can read English, and none under the age of fourteen. But who doesn't look the other way?"

"The laws of the future have changed," said the rabbi.

"Look," said Scroogemacher, "these children come from all different neighborhoods. It's a mishmash."

"In the future, all the children in America will be the sons and daughters of people who made a great journey, either long ago or not so long ago. They will not be divided by race or religion— and by class, maybe just a little."

"But these must all be children of some privilege," Scroogemacher said, scratching his head, "or would they not starve from such laws that keep them from working?"

"On the contrary, Mr. Scroogemacher! It is a privilege, yes, but a necessary one. They would more likely be hungry if they didn't go to school, and this is common knowledge."

"So all of these children can read and write and do sums?"

"Most all, yes." The rabbi smiled. "Or else they are learning. They have a chance at growing up to be whatever they dream of being, no matter their race or religion. Jews in America are doctors, lawyers, writers, athletes, performers . . . one even ran for vice president recently."

Scroogemacher whistled through his teeth. "The future is full of geniuses."

"Oh, yes." The rabbi smiled some more. "And do you know what that means? I will tell you. It means the days where bosses like you can live off of the toil of others are numbered, *kennehorra*."

"What do you mean?"

"So all of these children can read and write and do sums?"

Even as she spoke, the room seemed to grow hotter, and the terrible screams of women seemed to echo around them.

"In your near future, there will be a fire," said the rabbi, "at a factory." Even as she spoke, the room seemed to grow hotter, and the terrible screams of women seemed to echo around them. "Dozens upon dozens will perish in a terrible way. The only good thing to come of that nightmare day will be that it will be the end of such unsafe, unfair working conditions. People like Gerstein will rise up and no longer bend to the demands of men with the likes of your black heart."

"Not like that lightweight Gerstein!" Scroogemacher could not believe his ears.

"Yes, like Gerstein!" the rabbi insisted, pushing up her glasses. "You are a villain to those people, Mr. Scroogemacher! The workers will strike, they won't sew one stitch for you, and even though you think you can, you will not be able to fill their shoes. They will shout at the top of their lungs about their treatment, but you will be too much of a *dumkopf* to change. Your own nephew Moshe will try to help you do what is right, but again, the *dumkopf* thing." The rabbi shrugged.

"You dare to suggest I have no heart!"

"I dare to see what lies in store." The

rabbi calmly removed her glasses and squinted through them. "I see that you will also be insulted by your nephew's suggestion, and decide that you are not speaking to him anymore. He will move out, and that will be that. Kaput! He will go and live with his wife's family and work as a union organizer, trying to get people to ask for what they deserve. But the conditions will be so bad in his crowded tenement that he will die from typhus, and bring the sickness to all the children who live there as well."

"No!" Scroogemacher covered his ears, but he could hear her through his fingers.

"Meanwhile! Your business will fail, Mr. Scroogemacher, and you will die poor and lonely in a cold-water flat."

Scroogemacher stood with his mouth open so wide you could fit in a whole matzo ball. And why not? Wouldn't you be that shocked to hear such bad news?

"Or," said the rabbi.

"Or!" said Scroogemacher.

"Yes, or," repeated the rabbi.

"Or what?"

"*Or* is what we're here for," said the rabbi, wiping her glasses with a handkerchief and sliding them back up her nose. "We can go this way, or that way. Here, or there. Up, or down. Inside, or out."

"What is your point, Rabbi?"

"My point is, listen to your nephew. He thinks for the future. He will become a great union leader, a respected man. He will take over your business with your blessing, and your business will flourish and he will happily share the profits. Accept his bride, and they will come and live with you and be well. They will have children."

"They will?"

"See that *boychik*? There! He's your great-great-grand-nephew. Your very own bloodline, alive and well even a hundred years later."

Scroogemacher squinted. He looks a little like me when I was a boy, he thought. Yes, he does!

"Is he a good student?" asked Scroogemacher.

"In the middle." The rabbi sighed. "Not so good at spelling. Better at math."

"Spelling, shmelling," said Scroogemacher.

"He too will grow up to fight for working people. Even though children here and now are well taken care of, there are children all over the world who still work in sweatshops, as they did a hundred years ago, children who do not get the chance to go to school. There is still such a thing as slavery."

Scroogemacher and the rabbi watched as the bell rang, and his great-great-grand-nephew waited on the playground for his sister. They watched as the two children had a snowball fight with their friends. Even though their faces were all different colors and suggested many different countries, they played without the teasing or name-calling that Scroogemacher knew from the children's brawls on the streets of his time.

As they walked toward the children's homes, Scroogemacher

could not believe the things that met his eyes, and he spun like a dreidel, trying to take it all in. Cars and televisions. People talking on cell phones. Advertisements with women wearing bathing suits that made him cover his face in embarrassment, but that the children barely seemed to notice. Playgrounds, streetlights, and skyscrapers. And draping over all of it were the garlands and glitter of Christmas.

"Look at all these trees in the store windows!"

"Look at all these trees in the store windows!" shouted Scroogemacher.

shouted Scroogemacher. "Listen to the carols in the streets! What is this song, 'Jingle Bells'?"

"Christmas is a big part of America," the rabbi said, shrugging.

"It is a Christian holiday!" howled Scroogemacher. "I thought you said this country belonged to Jews as well as Christians, but everywhere, all I see is Christmas!"

"What can I say? They have good decorations."

"What sort of rabbi are you, anyway? If this loose talk is the future of Jewish generations, then perhaps it is best that fate plays itself out for me in the first way!"

"What do you care if they carry on Jewish tradition?" The rabbi stopped in her tracks. "Why are you making such a *tzimmes*? Weren't you the one who said 'Hanukkah, shmanukkah'?"

"But I was wrong!" cried Scroogemacher. "Look at the world my great-great-grand-nephew lives in, full of marvels. Electric trees. Double-stitched leather gloves, pictures that move in boxes, and carts that drive themselves."

"So? That's progress!"

"I'm not so sure. They don't seem to know where it all came from. Where are the Maccabees, who fought so bravely? And if they can't even remember that, then where are the huddled masses, yearning to breathe free? Where are the workers who endured such hunger so that someday their children could go to these fancy-shmancy schools? Where am *I*?" Scroogemacher howled.

"You? You're history," said the rabbi.

They followed the children up to their apartment. The children had their own rooms, where more screens glowed and rows of toys were lined up neatly on shelves. The father cooked in the kitchen, stirring soup and searing meat while he listened to the radio, and the mother soon stepped smartly through the door, carrying a briefcase, and kissed each member of the family.

The radiators clanged, and the sunset melted down in lines of pink and blue over the steaming rooftops.

And then, down from the shelf came the menorahs, one for each member of the family.

"Look! Look what they are doing!" Scroogemacher exclaimed.

The family gathered around the table. Out came the candles: one, two, for you; one, two, for you . . . and then the father and son put on yarmulkes and the mother began to sing, leading the prayer, her gentle breath making the fire-light flicker and dance.

"*Baruch atah Adonai . . .*"

"They do remember!" breathed Scroogemacher.

"Look! Look what they are doing!" Scroogemacher exclaimed.

"Baruch atah Adonai . . ."

"So they lit a few candles," said the rabbi.

"Candles, shmandles," said Scroogemacher. "Don't you see, it's not about the candles, it's about the remembering!"

"What are they remembering?" asked the rabbi.

"People," said Scroogemacher. "How hard people have worked to make their place in the world. Our people, and all people. Past, present, and future!"

The room glowed in the candlelight, and it seemed to Scroogemacher that the room began to swim before his eyes.

So then, this is what happened.

Scroogemacher woke up and said, "*Oy*, what a dream." He got out of bed and ate a cookie and poured some tea from the samovar and thought about what he remembered. Some of the things made him cry, and some of the things made him laugh.

He did not rush out and get a big challah and bring it to the Gersteins. What did you expect? That a leopard should change its spots?

But he unscrewed the dial in the wall that could turn back the clock in his sweatshop. He started to give with a warm hand a few pennies to the Hebrew Immigrant Aid society. When he got over the shock of the Triangle Factory fire, he listened to his nephew and gave the workers most of what they demanded. And when his nephew wanted to marry that Gerstein girl, he said, "Okay," and it turned out that they had a daughter whom they named Rose, even if her mother did look a little like a weed.

You see? Good things happen from a little remembering.

Especially on Hanukkah, shmanukkah.

AUTHOR'S NOTE

Why would I take a classic holiday story and rewrite it? Because that's what happens to stories; they change over time, as the people who tell them change. Storytellers add a pinch of salt here, a dash of pepper there. The iconic story of *A Christmas Carol* was one I wanted to flavor in my own way.

As funny as it may seem to turn a Christmas story into a Hanukkah story, it seemed a natural fit. What I always liked about Dickens's work was that his stories were often about people finding a home, a place where they belonged, a stature in a social system that was not always welcoming. Though he may not have intended it, these same themes reverberated in the lives of Jewish people during the mass migration of immigrants in America at the turn of the twentieth century. Guidance for these new arrivals could be found in *The Jewish Daily Forward*, a newspaper aimed at workers, encouraging them to form and join unions and helping them adapt to the ways of the *"Golden Medineh"* (golden land). This land was not always so golden for these struggling souls, however, as evidenced in "A Bintel Brief," a feature of the *Forward* in which the editor encouraged his readers to write about their daily lives. The letters poured in, giving insight into a plight that might very well be considered Dickensian:

1906
We work in a Bleecker Street shop, where we make raincoats. With us is a thirteen-year-old boy who works hard for the two and a half dollars a week he earns. Just lately it happened that the boy came to work ten minutes late. This was a "crime" the bosses couldn't overlook, and for the lost ten minutes they docked him two cents. Isn't that a bitter joke?

1906
This conscience of mine has a strong voice. It yells at me just as I yell at my workers, and scolds me for all my offenses against them. It will be enough for me to give just a few samples of my evil deeds: The clock in our shop gets "fixed" twice a day; the hands are moved back and forth. The foreman has on his table a stick like a conductor's baton and when someone says a word during working hours he hears the tick-tock of that stick....

    My conscience bothers me and I would like to correct my mistakes, so I do not have to be ashamed of myself in the future....

1908

We were sitting in the shop and working when the boss came over to one of us and said, "you ruined the work: you'll have to pay for it." The worker answered that it wasn't his fault, that he had given out the work in perfect condition. "You're trying to tell me!" The boss got mad and began to shout. "I pay your wages and you answer back, you dog! I should have thrown you out of my shop long ago."

The worker trembled, his face got whiter. When the boss noticed how his face paled, he gestured, spat, spat and walked away. The worker said no more. Tired, and overcome with shame, he turned back to his work and later he exclaimed, "For six years I've been working like a slave, and he tells me, You dog, I'll throw you out! I wanted to pick up an iron and smash his head in, but I saw before me my wife and five children who want to eat!"

Obviously, the offended man felt he had done wrong in not defending his honor as a worker and human being. In the shop, the machines hummed, the irons thumped, and we could see the tears running down his cheeks. . . .

To come to a new country, to assimilate, to deliver bread to one's family—all of these situations called upon the consciences of new immigrants to make an exhausting number of choices. Those who succeeded under such trying circumstances were expected to bring others along. People had to determine a balance between a secular lifestyle and traditional ways. These conflicts still stir in the hearts of those who come to America from all over the world. In *A Christmas Carol*, spirits abound to guide Scrooge in making decisions that help him to become a better man. Around me, too, I feel the spirits of these people who gave so much so I could live the life they dreamed of: a life of education, equality, and freedom. Using Dickens's structure, I tried to create a story for a modern audience that would shed light on a particular time and place in Jewish history. But even more so, I tried to create a story that, if the people of Hanukkah past could read what I had written, they would say, yes, yes, that's the way it was. And hopefully, good things really will happen from a little remembering.

—E. R. C.

A Short Glossary of Yiddish Words

Not to be confused with Hebrew, Yiddish is a language rooted in German that was widely used in the Jewish villages of Eastern Europe in the nineteenth century, and by Jewish immigrant groups who came to the *"Goldeneh Medineh"* in the early twentieth century. After six million Jews were killed in Europe during World War II, it was largely up to these immigrants to keep this language alive. But as many of their children became Americanized and assimilated into the culture in large part by speaking English, the use of Yiddish was largely reduced to a few energetic expressions, often used to share a strong feeling or opinion. Because there are several different dialects of Yiddish, there are many ways to pronounce and spell these words, just as there are many ways to spell Hanukkah! Try these words on your tongue and you will taste just a *bissell*—a little bit—of the flavor of Scroogemacher's time.

boychik (BOY-chick) little boy
bubbe (BUH-bee) grandmother
challah (KHOLL-ah) a loaf of bread, usually braided and made with eggs
chutzpah (KHOOTZ-pah) nerve
dreidel (DRAY-dl) a spinning top used by children to play a betting game at Hanukkah
dumkopf (DUM-ko) not a smart person
dybbuk (DIH-book) a demon or ghost; an evil spirit
farblondzhet (far-BLUN-jet) completely lost
farpatshket (far-POTSH-ket) sloppy, messy
farshtunkener (far-SHTOONK-uh-nuh) stinking
Gehenna (gih-HEN-uh) Hell
geshray (gush-RAY) to yell
gevalt (guh-VALT) help!
Goldeneh Medineh (GOL-din meh-DINE-uh) America; also means a hope that ends
    in disappointment
gonif (GO-niff) a thief
halvah (HOLL-vuh) a sweet treat made of honey and sesame paste
hoking a chainik (HOCK-ing a CHYI-nick) bothering someone by talking too much,
    giving some-one a headache; literally, "banging a kettle"
hotzeplotz (HUTZ-in-plutz) someplace far away
kaput (kuh-PUT) the end; broken; also means, It's over!
kennehorra (KIN-ih-HOR-uh) "no evil eye," an expression to ward off evil

kinder (KINN-der) children

kishkes (KISH-kee) intestines

klutz (klutz) a clumsy person

latkes (LAHT-kuhs) potato pancakes—good with sour cream or applesauce

makher (MAKH-her) a big shot (literally, "maker")

mazik (MAH-zick) cheerful mischief-maker

menorah (men-OR-uh) candelabra that holds nine candles, for each of the eight nights of Hanukkah, plus the *shammes*

mensch (mentsh) a good, decent person (literally, "human")

meshuggeh (meh-SHUH-geh) crazy

mishegas (MISH-ih-goss) melee, madness

nosh (nosh) a snack, a bite

nu (new) Well? So? Really? What else is new?

patshke (POTCH-key) play around

rabbi (RA-bye) teacher, leader in the Jewish community

shalom (shah-LOME) hello, peace

shammes (SHA-miss) candle used to light all the other candles on a Hanukkah menorah

shlep (shlep) to drag

shmatte (SHMA-tuh or SHMA-tee) a rag

shmendrick (SHMEN-drick) opposite of **mensch**

shtunk (shtoonk) a stinker, a nasty person

shvieg (shvyg) Be quiet!

tallis (TAHL-iss) prayer shawl

tsores monger (SOOR-iss MONG-ger) someone who likes to talk about sorrow and trouble

tzedakah (ze-DOCK-ah) charity

tzimmes (SIM-iss) a big deal, a fuss over a small thing

tuml (TOOM-l) noise

vey iz mir (VAYS-meer) my goodness

vildekinder (VIL-deh KIN-der) wild children

yarmulke (YAH-mull-keh) skullcap

zetz (zetz) punch, hit, or pinch

ILLUSTRATOR'S NOTE

Research for my illustrations for *Hanukkah, Shmanukkah!* began at my local Jewish Community Center, where I was given information on some of the traditions and customs of Jewish culture, from how to wear a tallis to the lighting of the menorah. I was also fortunate to do quite a bit of research in New York City, the setting of the story. Visiting the Lower East Side Tenement Museum enlightened me as to the immigrant experience at the turn of the century and beyond. The fascinating collection of photographs and objects and the tours of the real tenement apartments gave me a real-life setting upon which to base the story. At the Ellis Island Immigration Museum, I visited the site of the dramatic parting of Scroogemacher and his wife, and gathered valuable reference about the immigration process. In researching the Jewish experience in the United States, I am indebted to the following sources:

Bachrach, Susan D. *Tell Them We Remember: The Story of the Holocaust.* Boston: Little, Brown, 1994.

Bial, Raymond. *Immigrant Life on the Lower East Side.* Boston: Houghton Mifflin, 2002.

Black, Mary. *Old New York in Early Photographs.* 2nd rev. ed. New York: Dover Books, 1973.

Byron, Joseph, with Albert K. Baragwanath, Museum of the City of New York. *New York Life at the Turn of the Century in Photographs.* New York: Dover Books, 1985.

Charing, Douglas. *Eyewitness Books: Judaism.* 1st American ed. New York: Dorling Kindersley, 2003.

Grafton, John. *New York in the Nineteenth Century: 321 Engravings from Harper's Weekly and Other Contemporary Sources.* New York: Dover Books, 1977.

Granfield, Linda, and Arlene Alda. *97 Orchard Street, New York: Stories of Immigrant Life.* Plattsburgh, N.Y.: Tundra Books, 2001.

Riis, Jacob. *How the Other Half Lives: Studies Among the Tenements of New York.* New York: Dover Books, 1970.

Rochlin, Harriet, and Fred Rochlin. *Pioneer Jews: A New Life in the Far West.* Updated ed. Boston: Houghton Mifflin, 2000.

Sanders, Ronald, and Edmund V. Gillon, Jr. *The Lower East Side: A Guide to Its Jewish Past in 99 New Photographs.* New York: Dover Books, 1979.

Telushin, Rabbi Joseph. *The Golden Land: The Story of Jewish Immigration to America—An Interactive History with Removable Documents and Artifacts.* New York: Harmony, 2004.

The American–Israeli Cooperative Enterprise. The Jewish Virtual Library: *www.jewishvirtuallibrary.org.*

The Jewish Agency for Israel. The History of the Jewish People: *www.jewishhistory.org.il.*

—L. P.

FURTHER READING

Auch, Mary Jane. *Ashes of Roses*. New York: Henry Holt, 2002.

Bartoletti, Susan Campbell. *Kids on Strike!* Boston: Houghton Mifflin, 1999.

Bial, Raymond. *Tenement: Immigrant Life on the Lower East Side.* Boston: Houghton Mifflin, 2002.

Fishman, Cathy Goldberg. *On Hanukkah*. New York: Atheneum, 1998.

Freedman, Russell. *Immigrant Kids*. New York: Dutton, 1980.

Goldin, Barbara Diamond, and James Watling. *Fire! the Beginnings of the Labor Movement*. Reissue ed. New York: Puffin, 1997.

Hoobler, Dorothy and Thomas. *We Are Americans: Voices of the Immigrant Experience*. New York: Scholastic, 2003.

Metzker, Isaac, ed. *The Bintel Brief: Sixty Years of Letters from the Lower East Side to the Jewish Daily Forward*. Reissue ed. New York: Schocken Books, 1990.

Rosten, Leo. *The New Joys of Yiddish*. Updated ed. New York: Three Rivers, 2003.

Schotter, Roni. *Hanukkah!* Boston: Little, Brown, 1990.

Silverman, Maida. *Festival of Lights: The Story of Hanukkah*. New York: Aladdin, 1999.

Yerkow, Lila Perl. *The Great Ancestor Hunt: The Fun of Finding Out Who You Are*. Reprinted. New York: Clarion, 1990.